The Green Umbrella

The Green Umbrella

AND OTHER SPORTS STORIES
Compiled by the Editors
of
Highlights for Children

CONTENTS

THE GREEN UMBRELLA

By Carolyn Bowman

Meg dismounted from the uneven parallel bars and looked across the gym. She was so angry that her braids hurt. And it wasn't because her mother had woven them too tightly. "That Jennifer!" she said to her best friend, Flora.

"That Coach Appleby," said Flora. "*You* should have gotten the part."

The girls walked to the mat, where Jennifer was practicing. In just two weeks—on the night of the gymnastics show—Meg would take her turn on the uneven parallel bars. Jennifer would perform the Dancing Dragon. The routine, almost like a ballet, would be the highlight of the show.

Nearly everyone had tried out for it. But Meg had made her turn special. She'd brought her own green umbrella from home to use as a prop. She'd twirled it gracefully, then hidden behind it, then closed and opened it quickly.

Coach Appleby was pleased, and he'd added an umbrella to the routine, but he gave the part to Jennifer. "I need you on the uneven parallel bars, Meg," he'd said. "You're our own little butterfly."

But Meg wanted to be the dragon, and, "It's all so unfair," she said to Flora.

"Look out!" Flora said, as Jennifer tripped over her umbrella and fell.

Coach Appleby ran to the rescue. Making sure Jennifer was all right, he said, "You're having trouble with that last turn—Hey, Meg, can you come over here for a minute?"

Meg shrugged, made a sour-pickle face, and walked over.

"Show Jennifer how it's done, will you?"

Meg knew each step by heart. When the music began, she touched the umbrella to her forehead, then leaped into the routine. She opened the umbrella, crouched behind it, then peeked out at the few other girls in the class who were watching her routine. Spinning into the final turn, she leaped over the umbrella, then spun it in a wide arc over her head. The music ended, and she bowed to Jennifer, saying, "It's a cinch."

"Maybe for you." Jennifer went through the routine again. And fell. Again.

Coach Appleby helped her up. "Meg, you know all these moves so well. Maybe you could teach Jennifer."

Meg felt her braids tighten. "I . . . I can't. I've got to practice." She ran across the floor and leaped onto the uneven parallel bars, spinning faster and harder than ever before. But no amount of spinning could make her anger go away.

Flora waited for her to finish. "Jennifer will never get it right. Don't forget, she has to wear the dragon costume, and it will get in the way. Coach will be sorry he picked her instead of you."

In the days that followed, it looked as if Flora's prediction would come true. Jennifer continued to fall. Each time Flora would say, "I told you so," and each time Meg kept quiet. She didn't want to admit that she felt sorry for Jennifer. Jennifer was trying so hard. She was light on her feet, almost like fairy dust. But she just couldn't nail that last turn. And it looked as if she never would.

On dress rehearsal day, Meg watched Jennifer put on the dragon costume, a dark green leotard covered with scales. It had a short, fat tail that swung just so. Jennifer's face and hands were painted light green, and on her head was a pointed, green cap. The costume was adorable, Meg thought. She felt herself go green with envy, until the music started—until Jennifer tripped over her umbrella and fell.

"It's no use," Jennifer said, rubbing her knees and crying. "I can't do it."

"Yes, you can." Meg was surprised by the sound of her own voice. She helped Jennifer to her feet as Coach Appleby rushed over.

"That's it!" he said, "The umbrella has to go."

"What?" Meg couldn't believe what Coach was saying. The umbrella made the routine perfect. "I think I know what's wrong."

"You do?" Jennifer said, wiping her eyes.

"You do?" Coach Appleby repeated.

Meg looked at Jennifer's umbrella, measuring it against the girl, who was at least six inches shorter than she was. "Why didn't I think of it before? I'll be right back—don't move a muscle." Hurrying to her locker, she took out her own green umbrella.

For a moment, Meg cradled it in her arms. She had wanted to do the Dancing Dragon more than anything. Now, more than anything, she wanted the routine to succeed.

Back in the gym, she gave Jennifer her green umbrella. "Use this," she said. "It's smaller—just the right size for you. Now, about the turn . . ."

Meg waited for the music to begin. She was smiling. Her braids felt loose and comfortable. She watched Jennifer go through the Dancing Dragon routine. And this time, Jennifer got it right.

TEAMWORK

By David Lubar

After one week on the baseball team, Bobby knew that someone would make the obvious connection between his name and a piece of furniture. Sure enough, by the seventh day they were calling him "Bobby Benchwarmer," or "Bobby on the Bench," or other clever variations.

It had to happen, he thought, as he watched the game. He also knew that the name would eventually be shortened to "Bobby Bench," and then finally become just "Bench." It didn't bother him much, but he hoped the nickname would die out with the season and not follow him around for the next few years. A nickname could be as hard to shake off as a handful of glue.

"Look at that," he said to Peter, who was sitting next to him. "Chuck is still swinging too soon. If he doesn't change, he'll just keep fouling to the left."

"He always does that," Peter said. "But he's so good in the field that he gets to play most of the time. I wish I got to play more."

Bobby shrugged. He really didn't want to play the game. It was his parents' idea that he join the team. Bobby liked swimming and running, but he knew that baseball was the wrong sport for him. He enjoyed watching the game and found the strategy interesting, but he had the worst arm in the county. He could barely reach first from right field. He knew he could improve with practice, but he really wasn't interested. He thought it made more sense to work on skills he had than to get frustrated trying to develop skills he'd never really have. Still, it made his parents happy to see him playing on a team, and it gave him a good view of the game.

"I wish the coach would play you more," his dad said after the game. "Two innings isn't enough. How does he expect you to improve if you don't play?"

"That's OK, Dad," Bobby said. "I played enough." He could tell that his father was disappointed.

He was still thinking about this at the next game. "What's on your mind?" Coach Humphrey asked.

Bobby looked up. He liked the coach, but he knew it wasn't fair to ask for more time in the game. The coach had to do what was right for the team. In the lower grades, everyone got to play the same number of innings, but things changed at the higher levels. "Well, I'm fine, but my Dad wants me to play more."

The coach nodded. "All the dads do. Even the ones whose kids are in for most of the game. Ouch, look at that," he said, pointing toward the field. "Chuck is still fouling them. I tried to get him to wait."

"If he holds up his swing, it will throw off his timing. Just tell him to start with the bat farther back," Bobby said.

"What?"

"It's hard to change your timing. But if he starts with his bat a bit farther back, he'll get the same result. The bat has to travel farther. He can start his swing at the same time and still hit the ball a bit later."

"I'll be right back," the coach said. He ran over to the backstop and motioned to Chuck. Then he

15

whispered something to him. Chuck looked surprised at first. Then he nodded. The coach came
back to the bench. He and Bobby watched as
Chuck nailed the next pitch for a line-drive double.

"Where'd you learn that?" the coach asked.

Bobby shrugged. "I don't know. I watch a lot. I
read a bit. You know . . . "

"Any other hints?" the coach asked.

"Yeah, don't play Tony at shortstop. He belongs
on second. In his head, he'll always be playing
second. When he's at shortstop, he always takes
longer before making the throw." Bobby stopped.
He didn't want to be rude and tell the coach what
to do. "Sorry."

"No, that's fine. You're absolutely right. I
noticed he seemed to bobble a bit, but I wasn't
sure what was going on."

After the game, Bobby's dad said, "You played
just one inning. It doesn't seem fair."

"It was fine," Bobby told him. "I had a good
time." He realized he had really enjoyed that
game. He changed to his running clothes and
went out for some exercise.

At the start of the next game, the coach walked
up to him and said, "You're out of uniform, Bobby."

"What?" Bobby looked down. He was wearing
his uniform.

"Here, put this on." The coach handed him a jacket. Bobby looked at the back. There, in white letters on the blue cloth, it said, "Assistant Coach."

"Assistant?" Bobby asked. "Me?"

The coach nodded. "You know the game. You see things a lot of other people would miss. I could use the help. Of course, you won't get as much playing time. Do you think your dad would understand?"

Bobby held up the jacket and looked at his parents in the stands. His father was talking excitedly to his mother and pointing over to Bobby. Then he saw his father talking to the man next to him, and then to the woman behind him, and then to everyone else in the stands.

"I think this will work," Bobby said, slipping into the jacket. He looked back at the game. "Have you noticed that Chris always throws low and inside to a left-handed batter? I think the other team is beginning to catch on. Now, here's how we take advantage of this."

For the rest of the game, and the rest of the season, Assistant Coach Bobby Benchley, known briefly as "Bench," stood in front of that piece of furniture and talked game-time strategy with Coach Humphrey.

Pride
of the
Lake

By Diane Burns

Pride of the lake. Pride of the lake. Boone's hiking boots clumped their rhythm on the storm-washed mountain shore. He caressed his fly pole. Today, the Pride of the Lake—the legendary "uncatchable" fish of Clear Lake—would meet its match. He and Dad had hiked for hours to spend their last day of vacation here. Not to kill the Pride of the Lake—never to kill it. This wilderness lake was a catch-and-release fisherman's dream— Boone's dream come true.

"Remember, son, we start back in three hours." Dad waved as he headed upshore. "Use your time well."

Boone nodded. Midday sun beckoned on the water, and the waves called to him with a gentle music. As Boone stepped across a pebble-lined bank a few feet from the lakeshore, he spotted a fingerling trout finning desperately in the shallow-water trap. *Probably it had been swept there during last night's storm*, Boone reasoned. The *how* didn't really matter, though. The important thing was the little fish was trapped and would die unless somehow it was caught and then released back into the lake.

Boone hesitated. He'd need all three hours to fish the rim of Clear Lake. There wasn't time to chase this baby fish, not if he hoped to catch and release the Pride of the Lake. Boone turned his attention to Clear Lake.

As if to tease him, a fat rainbow trout swam past, just offshore. Boone dropped his backpack on the beach and swung his fishing pole in a practiced arc; the line sailed out into the deep water. His fly pole sang and danced its fish-catching tune, but the big trout didn't even give Boone's fly a second look.

No matter, Boone told himself. Surely the Pride of the Lake was larger than this trout. A shadow followed in the wake of the first fish. Again Boone swung his line, but the gliding shape was only a trout no bigger than Boone's hand. Not much bigger than the fingerling still trapped in the shallow-water pool.

Boone bit his lip. That fingerling again! He was wasting precious time thinking about it. Another fat rainbow cruised by, but Boone didn't notice. He was standing over the pool, watching the panicked fingerling dart to and fro. *Catch and release,* Boone thought. *Fish for the future. This one wouldn't have a future unless . . .*

Boone squared his shoulders and sighed. It was up to him. Dad was on the opposite shore, too far away to help. Alone, he'd have to try his own catch-and-release rescue. Boone kicked off his hiking shoes and socks and rolled up his jeans. He waded into the icy pool, but the little trout scooted away from his cupped hands. Boone chased the fish around and around while precious minutes sped by. After a half hour, his feet were numb.

"S-s-stupid fish," Boone chattered with cold. "I'm trying to save your neck." No, that didn't sound right, so he said, "I'm trying to save your fins."

The fish, with its wily eye, stared up at him.

"You're too fast to chase," Boone said. "I'll have to outwit you."

He splashed out of the pool and lay at the edge with his arms dangling over. He cupped his hands at the bottom. He held perfectly still. Minutes passed. A Canada jay, perched on a nearby branch, shrilled bits of harsh advice, and wildflowers nodded encouragement as Boone waited patiently for a half hour. And another. Slowly, slowly, the trout finned its way closer. Boone bit his lip and waited . . . waited . . . now!

Boone grabbed, but the fish darted away. Boone glanced at his watch in frustration. His fishing time was nearly gone!

"I need something bigger than my hands," Boone told the wary fingerling. "Or at least something sneakier." He sighed. This wouldn't be easy. Wily-Eye was good at avoiding man-traps. While the remaining minutes passed, Boone sat and thought and thought.

Finally, Boone spied his fly rod. "I don't want to hook you, Wily-Eye. But I don't have a choice. You're too smart to fall for anything else."

Boone dangled the line and fly over the edge of the bank. Carefully, he lowered it until the fly hovered just an inch above the water line in the shallow pool. He waited. Wily-Eye turned, spotted the insect, and SNAP! In the flick of a fin, he'd captured the fly.

Boone held the line and its flopping prize and hightailed it for the beach. The fish was hooked only by its lip. Good!

Wily-Eye gasped and his eye met Boone's. He would remember this man-trap.

Boone lay at the beach's edge. His hands moved quickly and gently to remove the hook. "Grow fat, Wily-Eye," he whispered. "Remember the feel of this trap. I'll see you again."

Boone opened his hands. Wily-Eye finned, righted himself in the lapping waves, and eyed Boone one more time. "You'll be worth the wait, Little Pride of the Lake," Boone said. "It'll be an even match next time."

There was a crunch of boots on beach gravel behind him. Dad said, "It's time to go, son. Looks as if neither of us met the Pride of the Lake after all."

Boone watched as a tiny ripple spread from Wily-Eye's wake. "Next time," he said. "He'll be right here waiting for me . . . the next time."

Briana's Blades

by Virginia L. Kroll

Briana slunk to the breakfast table and slumped into her chair. Her shoulders told Mama just how she felt.

"What is it?" Mama asked. A ladle dripping with hot oatmeal hovered in her hand.

"Look at the frost ferns decorating the window," Briana said. "Delaware Park Lake is frozen solid for sure, and my skates are only good for last year's feet." Her voice had a wobble in it.

Mama's mouth smiled but her eyes didn't. "You've grown some," she said.

"Mama?" Briana said.

"Yes, Baby?"

"Oh, nothing." Money was even tighter than her skates. Briana changed her mind about asking for new ones and ate her oatmeal in silence.

James eased in front of a heaping bowl. "Looks like winter whooshed in behind our very backs," he said.

"Right in front of our very eyes, except we weren't awake to see it," Mama said.

Briana excused herself and went to her room. "Enough of that 'winter talk' for me. Does me no good, nohow."

Briana pouted for a while.

"I'll earn new blades," she suddenly decided. Briana got dressed fast and headed out the door.

That very afternoon, Briana got busy. She shoveled the Johnsons' driveway and walked Mrs. Jenkins's dog because Mrs. Jenkins didn't do well on the ice. On Tuesday she helped Mrs. Otis in her sewing shop after school, and on Friday she watched the little Steele girls in their fenced-in yard. Every chance she got in between, Briana went to the frozen lake to slide on her imaginary skates. Several weeks went by.

One evening Briana counted her money. She shuffled to supper with a lump in her throat. Her drooping cheeks told Mama just how she felt.

"What is it?" Mama asked.

"The races are just two days away, and I don't even have enough money for secondhand skates." Briana's voice was wobbly again.

James eased into his usual place. "Get that rubber band out of your voice, Briana. Here." He slid a battered box across the table.

Briana peeked under the lid. "Oh," she whispered, opening the box.

"Used to be mine. I've grown some, too," James said with laugh. "They're not the right color, but they are blades, and they sure know their way around Delaware Park Lake."

Mama said, "James, you were supposed to sell them to help with the money for your senior class ring."

"Oh, I'll just wait a little. The ring is almost paid for. And anyway," he said, "this finger doesn't need a ring right now as bad as these feet need skates." He grabbed Briana's toes, and she giggled.

Mama said, "Can you imagine that?" Now her voice was rubber band wiggly.

Briana flung her arms around James's neck, gulped her stew, and grabbed her jacket.

"Where do you think you're going?" Mama asked.

"I've got to practice," Briana said.

"I'll take her, Mama," James offered, grabbing his jacket, too.

"Hat and gloves!" Mama called.

Briana covered her head and hands, slung the skates over her shoulder, and bounded down the apartment steps. James shoved his hands deep into his pockets and turtled his neck into his collar.

The floodlights were on. Briana sat on the slatted bench and slid into her jet-black skates. She tugged and tied the laces until they felt just right.

She paused and stared at her skate-clad feet.

Briana made her way to the ice. She pushed off and began to glide.

Marvin sailed by, his voice trailing behind him. "Hey Briana, black skates are for boys!"

"Black skates are for skating!" she shouted.

Her silver blades cut sharp white shapes into the crystal surface. Sometimes they wrote her name in cursive. Briana skated until the floodlights were off and James said, "I've got homework and you've got bed."

The morning of the races came. Folks were blowing breath balloons and pacing, trying to keep warm.

Skaters lined up in nervous rows. Red triangle flags and orange cones decorated the ice. Briana spotted Mama's puffing cheeks and James's "thumbs up" sign.

A whistle blew. Watches ticked. An announcer's voice blared from a scratchy speaker. Briana's cheeks flushed. She got on her mark. She got set. A whistle blew. Briana flew!

She sailed and she soared. She was wind and rain and lightning together.

She snapped the ribbon at the finish line. Then she spun around to make sure that she was really first. Applause crackled in the air. The judges shook her hand. Briana thanked them and zoomed away.

"Mama! James!" she panted. "Look what my black skates and I won." She held up her gold award proudly.

"You were gone, Baby!" Mama said.

"An awesome blur!" James added.

They celebrated with hot chocolate at Becker's Cafe. "To Briana. Go for the gold," James toasted with his steaming mug.

Briana pulled a box from her pocket and slid it across the table. "Here."

James peeked in under the lid. "Oh," he whispered, smiling.

"I almost had enough, then Mama helped me out," Briana laughed. "I didn't need the money because I already had skates."

James took his senior class ring out of the box and slid it onto his finger. For a moment he paused and stared at his ring. Then he clicked the ring against Briana's trophy.

"Go for the gold!" he said again.

Mama said, "Imagine that . . ." The glint in her eyes filled the whole cafe with the coziest kind of glow.

The Champion of Miller's Lane

By Michael David Hardy

Derek Barnes adjusted the straps of his helmet, straightened his sunglasses, and pulled on his black leather gloves, stretching his fingers for a snug fit.

Derek, the defending champion of the Miller's Lane bike race, looked to his left at the crowd of eager bikers hoping to strip him of his title.

"You ready, D.B.?" asked Joey Mains, Derek's longtime friend and neighbor.

"You bet! We couldn't have practiced any harder." Derek smiled and pushed the hair from his eyes.

"Yeah," Joey agreed. "And this time *I'm* gonna beat *you.*"

Derek just laughed. "We'll see. Let's do it."

Joey slipped a pair of motorcycle goggles over his eyes. He turned to Derek, who was trying hard not to laugh. "What? So maybe I like wearing goggles, OK?" Derek smiled and gave Joey the "thumbs up." Joey returned the smile.

"On your mark," announced the starter. "Get set . . . *Go!*" The small crowd cheered as the bikers bolted from the line.

The pack of racers stayed close together as they left the school and sped along the Congress Street bike lane. Derek, pedaling comfortably, positioned himself just behind the leaders and waited for the right time to move.

Derek gripped his handlebars tightly, pumping the sleek, red bicycle past the bus stop that marked the halfway point of the two-mile race. He glanced to his right and gave Joey a nod.

Both boys burst from the pack and quickly overtook the leaders, who had used much of their energy in the early going. Derek and Joey pedaled furiously as they battled for the lead. Derek got the inside track as they screamed around Buttermilk Curve, and he pulled to the front.

The panting racers, now forming two packs

rather than one, quickly approached the covered footbridge. The bridge's wooden planks rumbled as the bikers zipped across the narrow span. Derek could feel the thumping of the uneven boards vibrate up his arms. This part of the course always made his ears tickle.

Bolting from the bridge into the hot afternoon sun, Derek leaned hard into the sharp right turn, looking over his shoulder to check the competition. Joey and two others were hot on his trail like hounds after a fox. Most of the others had fallen behind.

Derek barely slowed down as he turned onto Miller's Lane and flew past a small group of kids who had gathered to watch the racers go by. He was on the homestretch now, but he knew he couldn't let up.

Sweat stung his eyes as he steered his bike around the last sharp corner before Pop's Dairy Delight and the finish line. Again he turned his head to check the other riders. He had put a little more distance between himself and Joey, who seemed to have second place all but wrapped up.

Suddenly Joey's bike started shaking uncontrollably. Derek watched in horror as it lurched to the right and hit the curb sharply, launching Joey through the air like a football.

The finish line was just ahead, but Derek slammed on his brakes, leaving a long, black tire mark on the pavement. He spun the bike around and went like a shot back up the street.

"Joey! Hey, Joey, are you OK?" Derek jumped off his bike and let it fall to the ground. Joey lay crumpled on the sidewalk, holding his scraped and bleeding right arm. A couple of other riders had stopped, and one of them ran to a house to call an ambulance.

"My arm, my shoulder, something's wrong with my shoulder," Joey said. "I think it must be broken, or out of joint, or . . ."

"Don't try to get up," said Derek. "Someone will be here pretty quick; just lie there and take it easy."

Joey lifted his arm slightly, winced, and put his head back on the sidewalk.

"It seems to move OK," Derek said. Joey nodded, eyes closed. Derek could see that he was in a lot of pain, but he didn't dare move him before the ambulance got there.

"Not exactly like we practiced, was it?" Joey joked, laughing weakly.

"Not exactly," Derek said. He pulled his T-shirt off and made a faded green pillow for his friend's head.

"Man, you really had us beat, D.B.," Joey said, opening his eyes. "Thanks for coming back to help."

"No sweat," Derek said, gently gripping Joey's hand. "We'll get 'em next year."

Maisie Winter Does It Again

By F.C. Nicholson

"Oh sure, I love to ski," I said.

Jeanne smiled at me, showing perfect teeth. "Excellent! I haven't been skiing since we moved here. It will be great to have someone to ski with again!"

It would be great, I thought, *if I knew how to ski.*

The other girls who were crowded around Jeanne's lunch table stared at me. Sue wanted to ask me when I had learned, I could tell. But as she opened her mouth, the bell rang.

I fiddled with my tray to let the others go, but Jeanne stayed behind. "Let's go Sunday. My dad will drive us."

"I, uh, I have to ask my mom."

"OK. Call me." She scribbled her phone number on a scrap of paper. "Gotta run!" She hurried away.

How desperate was I, I wondered, to impress the new kid in school? Jeanne had just moved to our little Massachusetts town from Colorado. She had told us all about the ski lodge her dad had owned, and how her brother was a champion. She'd won some skiing competitions, too. All I'd ever won was a third-grade spelling bee. And that was just because Sue left the first *r* out of *aardvark*.

When classes ended, I rushed home to talk to Mom. She works at home designing brochures and pamphlets and stuff on her computer.

"Mom!" I dropped my books on the kitchen counter with a slam and went looking for her. She was in the den. She swiveled her chair and looked at me from over the rims of her glasses.

"Good thing I'm not a sculptor," she said. "That crash would have cost me a month's work."

"Sorry," I said. "But I've got good news. The most popular girl in fifth grade wants to be friends with me!"

"Is that so?" Mom frowned at her computer.

"Mom! Did you hear me? Jeanne Roebling wants me to go skiing with her Sunday!"

"Skiing? Honey, you don't ski. You don't even like to ice-skate."

"I can learn," I said defensively.

"In a day?"

"And a half. Can we please go to Mount Wachusett before Sunday?"

"Maisie, I'm sorry. I've got to get this pamphlet done by tomorrow noon, and tonight Aunt Alice is coming for dinner. This weekend's just impossible."

On Saturday I went to the library. When I asked for a book on skiing, the librarian said, "Trying another sport, Maisie?"

I blushed. "Yeah. The horseback riding, uh, didn't work out." After weeks of bugging my mom for lessons, I'd been too scared to get on the horse.

All the skiing books were out. "How about ice-skating?" the librarian suggested. I just shook my head.

Sunday arrived. I still didn't know how to ski. *Maisie Winter*, I thought, *you've done it again*. Jeanne and her dad drove up in a blue Jeep. Mr. Roebling was a big, bearded man with a deep chuckle. Mom waved good-bye. "Good luck, Maisie," she said.

The sun was bright, and its reflection off the snow was blinding. Jeanne had wraparound goggles with hot pink frames that matched her jacket that matched her pants that matched the bag that held her skis. I had a pair of my Mom's nylon jogging pants over my jeans. At least I had a ski jacket.

I rented skis and clunky boots. I watched Jeanne as she put hers on and I did just the same, a motion behind. Jeanne and her dad glided across the snow toward the lift. I didn't glide. I felt like I was roller-skating on two giant fence pickets.

Mr. Roebling caught the chair lift, and we waited for the next. It caught me offguard, whacking the backs of my legs. "Oof!" I said.

"You OK?" Jeanne asked.

"Fine, fine." But my legs still stung. My feet dangled in the air. It was a long way—a long, long way—from the chair lift to the ground. I looked at the sky, at Mr. Roebling's back, at Jeanne—anywhere but down.

I told my dad you know how to ski," Jeanne said. "So we figured we'd do an expert trail for the first run."

"Uh, shouldn't we start off slow?"

She looked at me quizzically. "Slow? Half the fun of skiing is speed! Hey, look out!"

The lift had just reached the top of the mountain, and as it set down, the tips of my skis jammed into the snow. I somersaulted out of the lift. Mr. Roebling and the lift attendant helped me up. "I'm OK," I said weakly, brushing snow out of my face.

"OK, let's go!" Jeanne started off toward the steep, bumpy trail for experts.

Maybe the fall off the lift scared me, I don't know. "Wait!" I heard myself say. They looked back at me.

I shrugged and admitted, "I don't really know how to ski. I thought if I said I did, well, Jeanne, I thought you'd like me and want to be friends." As I spoke I felt stupid, but relieved, too.

Jeanne glided back to me. "Maisie, I do like you. I like skiing, too. Maybe I can teach you—since you've got the skis rented and all." She turned to her father. "See you at the bottom, Dad! We're going to start slowly, on the bunny slope." He waved and disappeared down the expert trail.

"Now, just bend your knees and push with your poles," Jeanne said to me.

As we glided down the gentle slope, I thought, *Maisie Winter, you've done it—right.*

The Boy Who Swam the Golden Gate

By Jeffrey Allen

Ted and his grandfather sat on the beach in Golden Gate Park, tossing stones into the water. They had strolled down from Chestnut Street to watch the sailboats in San Francisco Bay.

It was a magical summer day—sunny and clear. The fog was hours away.

As he sat on the beach, Ted marveled at the men and women who swam around the cove. "Why do all the swimmers wear bright orange caps?" he asked his grandfather.

"So they can be seen by boats and lifeguards," Grandad said. "The color is called international orange. And the Golden Gate Bridge is international orange, too."

Ted picked up another stone and tossed it high over the water.

"I wonder how cold that water is," Ted said. He rolled up his jeans and walked to the edge of the bay.

"Hey, Grandad," Ted called. "It feels OK."

But the cold soon bit into Ted's feet, and he jogged back up the beach to Grandad.

"Those orange caps help keep the swimmers warm," Grandad said. "Some of them swim the length of the Golden Gate Channel, right under the bridge."

"Wow!" Ted said. "What about sharks?"

"Well, there are sharks in San Francisco Bay, but not the kind that eat you," Grandad said. "The biggest problems for the swimmers are the cold and the currents. You could be swept right out to sea!"

"I'll bet I could swim the Golden Gate," Ted said.

It takes lots of training," Grandad said. "Many years ago, there was an eleven-year-old boy who swam the Golden Gate."

"That's only three years older than I am!" Ted's eyes grew big with wonder. He knew his grandfather was about to tell one of his stories.

"That boy trained very hard," Grandad said. "Every day, after school, his dad brought him to the South End Rowing Club to train. At first, he could only stand being in the water for ten minutes—it was that cold. But then he grew used to it and he could stay in longer, up to an hour. He wasn't the greatest swimmer, but I guess that young lad had something to prove."

"Did he make it?" Ted asked.

Grandad chuckled, then he grew serious. He always got serious when he told Ted a story.

"It was rainy and cold the day that boy swam the Golden Gate," Grandad said. "His dad got him up at five in the morning. He packed warm clothes, and they walked to the South End Club. The boy and his dad rode a kayak out to the bridge. Odde, a big, ruddy man who took care of the club's boats, was in another kayak."

Grandad gazed out into the bay for a moment, then continued his story. "It was still dark as the two kayaks set out. A big luxury liner with bright lights passed silently in the dark. Against the big ship, the kayaks looked like little toys.

"The kayaks reached a rock at Fort Baker in Marin. The boy took off his rain-soaked sweatshirt and jeans to swim the mile and a quarter south to Fort Point in San Francisco.

"In the dark, early silence the boy could hear cars swishing by overhead. 'Let's go!' his father yelled.

"The boy, wearing just a swimsuit, goggles, and a bright orange cap, began to swim. His father and Odde followed closely in the boats.

"His strokes were long and strong: right arm, left arm, right arm, left . . .

"He heard himself breathing and saw the dark water surrounding him. Left arm, right arm, left arm, right . . .

"'More to the east!' Odde shouted. 'Head to the east!' The current was pulling the boy out of the bay toward the Pacific Ocean.

"The boy worked harder and quickly got back on course. Then he slowed and took a look toward the shore. He had already swum half the distance. 'This isn't so bad,' he thought.

"But soon the boy's legs began to tingle. His arms felt heavy. When he opened his mouth to breathe, his jaw ached. 'I'm getting cold,' he said to himself.

"The water seemed to rise up around him. For as far as he could see, there was nothing but water. Miles and miles of water.

"He continued to swim, but now he felt so alone. It was just him, the water, and the bridge. All he heard for the longest time was his breath and the movement of his arms through the water.

"Suddenly he looked up. There was his father, right above him, leaning from the kayak. 'We've been yelling at you for five minutes!' his dad said. 'The current has changed! Swim to the west now. You're not far from the beach! Go west!'

"His dad's voice gave him strength. Right arm, left arm—he headed toward the beach.

"Soon he felt his feet dragging in the sand. He stood on his weak legs, fell into the knee-deep water, and stood again. He looked back across the bay.

"There was the bridge, just as it had always been. The sun began to break through the gray morning clouds.

Then he was on the beach, and his father handed him a towel. Odde was holding a cup of hot chocolate for him.

"'Congratulations!' Odde said. He handed the boy the cup.

"'Nice going!' his dad said.

"The boy dressed, and soon the three of them kayaked back to the club. Odde paddled while the boy rested, gazing at the bridge behind him."

Grandad's story was over. He stood up, stretched, and brushed the sand from his pants. Ted sat quietly on the beach. He wondered if he'd ever swim the Golden Gate.

And where was the boy who had done it?

"Grandad," Ted asked, "was the boy who swam the Golden Gate actually *you?*"

Grandad just smiled. He took Ted's hand, and the two walked back up toward Chestnut Street.

I Really Need Batting Practice

By Marilyn Kratz

"Guess what, Mom!" called Chad, bursting into the kitchen. "There's going to be a day camp for batting practice at the park next week. May I go, Mom, please?"

"I'm sorry, dear," said Mom. "I promised Grandma and Grandpa that you and I would spend next week with them at their cabin in the woods."

"But, Mom! I really need batting practice," protested Chad. "Couldn't I stay home with Dad?"

"Your father will be away next week on a business trip," said Mom. "That's why I decided we'd go to the cabin. It seemed like the perfect time."

"But, Mom!" Chad repeated. He sank onto a kitchen stool, trying to think of another argument.

"I wish you could go to the batting camp," said Mom, putting her arm around Chad. "But I can't leave you here alone. Besides, Grandpa would be so disappointed if you didn't come. You know how he loves to take you fishing."

"Yeah," muttered Chad, sliding off the stool. "I guess I'd better start packing."

Chad went to his room, but he didn't get out his suitcase. Instead, he sprawled across his bed, wondering about the strange feelings inside him. Every other year he had been anxious to go fishing with Grandpa. But this year nothing seemed as important as working on his batting.

Chad tried to be cheerful on the way to the cabin. He felt a twinge of guilt when they arrived, and Grandpa greeted him joyfully.

"The fish are really biting this year, Chad," said Grandpa. "I'll bet we get our limit every day. Did you bring your lucky fishing hat?"

"Uh, no, I didn't," Chad mumbled. Then he quickly changed the subject. "We'd better unload these suticases and start unpacking."

Chad was the last one up the next morning. When he ambled into the kitchen, everyone else was already eating Grandma's fluffy buckwheat cakes dripping with homemade blackberry syrup.

"We saved you a mile-high stack, Chad," teased Grandpa. "You'll need lots of energy today. Your Grandma plans to put us to work before we get to go fishing."

"Now, John," said Grandma. "You have neglected those little jobs long enough. You know this is our last week here this summer."

Chad dug into his pile of buckwheat cakes, feeling relieved to have the fishing put off for at least a while. "What's the first job, Grandma?"

"Well, I hardly know where to have you start," said Grandma. "The screen door needs fixing, the back steps are sagging, and there's that mess of acorns under the oak tree out back."

"Don't the squirrels eat those acorns?" asked Chad between mouthfuls.

"They take some of them," said Grandma. "But the tree produced so many this year. And lots of them fell last week in that windstorm. If they aren't picked up, they'll sprout next spring and ruin our back clearing."

"I'll pick them up," Chad offered. "What should I do with them?"

"Carry them into the woods at the edge of the clearing," said Grandma.

After breakfast, Grandma gave Chad a small bucket, and he began to gather the acorns. It was slow, tedious work. After a while, Chad set the bucket down and practiced pitching acorns into it. Suddenly, he had an idea. He ran to Grandpa who was working on the back steps.

"Grandpa, may I use this flat board?" he asked, picking up a piece of wood.

"Sure," said Grandpa. "But how will that help you with your job?"

"Just watch!" shouted Chad. He picked up an acorn, tossed it over his head, and as it fell, he batted it far into the woods.

"Home run!" shouted Grandpa, laughing. "Let's see you do that again!"

Grandpa watched while Chad batted more acorns into the woods, missing only a few.

"You're as good a batter as your dad was when he was a boy," said Grandpa, walking over to Chad. "Shall I toss you a few?"

The speed at which Grandpa tossed the acorns surprised Chad. He hit only about half of them.

"I really need batting practice," said Chad, when they stopped to rest for a minute. "I'd like to make it onto a league team next year."

"I wish you had brought along your ball and bat," said Grandpa. "I could help you practice."

"I did bring them, Grandpa!" exclaimed Chad. "They're in the trunk of the car."

"Well, run and get them, my boy!" said Grandpa, his eyes twinkling. "We have some practicing to do."

"What about the rest of our jobs—and fishing?" asked Chad.

"Oh, they'll keep," said Grandpa, chuckling. "After all, we have the whole week."

Chad gave his grandfather a quick hug. "It's going to be a great week," he said.

One-Man Team

By Carol Reinsma

Mark pulled off his helmet and ran his hands through his damp hair. "I quit," he said.

His teammates straggled off the ice and plopped onto the bench. "We're the worst team in the league," Mark said.

Graham thrust a finger at Mark. "What team?" he said. "You seem to think it's a one-man team."

Mark stared at the ice. "What a bunch of losers," he mumbled. "We haven't scored all season."

Coach Casey motioned everyone to gather around. "Listen up, guys," he said. "That team had strong skaters and they played together well. When we start playing like a team, we'll start winning."

Mark took off his padded gloves. "Fat chance," he muttered.

The players stuffed their gear into their oversized duffel bags. Mark started to leave, but the coach called him back. "Let's talk a minute," he said.

Great, thought Mark. *Here it comes.*

Coach twisted his whistle cord. "You were chosen captain because I thought you'd be a leader."

Mark felt his eyes burn. "If they'd pass the puck to me, maybe I could score."

"I'm not talking about scoring," Coach said. "You need to be the one who helps this team work together."

Mark started to protest, but Coach put up his hand. "Just think about it," he said.

Mark shouldered his bag. He slowly followed the curve of the rink and went out the double doors.

The snow had started falling, but Mark didn't wait in the bus shelter with Graham and the others. He stood in the falling snow.

Warming up for the next game, the Beavers seemed to have a burst of enthusiasm. They dug their skates into the ice and skated hard across the arena. *Whack!* Pucks crashed against the boards.

When Coach Casey blew the whistle, the players skated to the net. "Take a knee," he said.

Mark kneeled outside the circle of teammates.

"You look strong today," Coach told them. "Remember to hustle and pass that puck."

"And pick up your feet," Mark said. "You slide like Bambi on the ice."

The words echoed across the arena.

"Mark," Coach said, "remarks like that don't help the team. You'll sit out the first period."

Mark skated to the bench and sat with his head between his gloves.

The referee dropped the puck at center ice, and the players burst into action. The Hawks' center took control of the puck and skated down the ice. He flicked it toward the front of the goal, but Graham intercepted it.

"Good defense," Mark said.

"It was," Coach said. "Let's hope our forwards will work together now."

Mark unraveled a piece of tape on his stick. *They don't have to work together*, he thought. *They just have to learn how to shoot.*

Kevin had taken control of the puck and was skating toward the goal, trying to break through a line of Hawks defensemen. It didn't work. The puck squirted loose and the Hawks recovered it.

"Graham was open!" Mark shouted.

The Hawks worked up the ice, passing the puck from one player to another. As one player shot, others raced toward the goal. The Beavers' goalie blocked the shot, but the rebound was fired past his outstretched stick. The Hawks had scored.

"Coach," Mark said. "If Kevin and Graham would pass to each other, they would have a better chance."

"That's right," Coach Casey said. "Maybe it isn't so easy to notice when you're out there on the ice, but it's been our biggest problem all season."

Mark ran his finger over the patch on his purple jersey. He traced the glossy "C" that stood for captain. "You mean my problem," he muttered.

The buzzer sounded to end the first period. The Beavers skated slowly to the bench.

"Let's show some teamwork out there," Coach Casey said.

Mark took a long sip from his water bottle. "I'll pass to you guys if you'll do the same for me."

Graham hitched up his socks. "Sure," he said with a frown. "Anything to make you the star."

"Give it a break," Kevin said. "We've all been hogging the puck."

The Beavers huddled together. They stacked their hands in a pile. "Teamwork," said the coach. "Teamwork!" the players hollered.

The Beavers started playing better, but the Hawks' tough defense kept them from mounting much of an attack. With less than a minute remaining in the game, the Hawks were ahead, 3-0, and were working toward the goal again. Suddenly, Graham knocked the puck away. He flipped a pass to Kevin, who skated along the boards and up the ice.

Mark raced toward center ice, zeroing in on the goal. "Kevin!" he shouted.

Kevin dodged past a defender and slid the puck to Mark. The angle was perfect. Mark got set to shoot, lifting his stick and leaning toward the goal. *Finally*, he told himself. *This is it.*

The goalie shifted position and cut off the left side of the goal. Out of the corner of his eye, Mark could see Graham skating in from his right.

The cry of "Teamwork!" seemed to echo in Mark's head.

There was no more time to think. Mark faked with his head, then slapped the puck hard over to Graham.

The smooth, black puck went soaring into the net. Goal!

Graham raised his stick above his head in a triumphant gesture.

"We broke our streak of zeros!" yelled Kevin.

The Beavers rushed over to Graham, pounding his back and whooping.

Graham slipped from the mob and slapped hands with Mark. "We sure caught that goalie off guard," he said.

The final buzzer sounded, and the players skated off the ice.

Mark looked up at the scoreboard, then followed his teammates toward the lockers. The puck sat on the blue line, and Mark slapped it into the goal.

Smooth, he thought as he watched the puck ripple the net. *Maybe we're a team after all.*

Captain's Choice

By David Hill

The last time we played Kerry Swag's basketball team, Kerry nailed a long jump shot at the buzzer to beat us. Last fall she threw three touchdown passes to beat us in the girls' flag football championship. And earlier this winter she scored three goals to knock us right out of the indoor soccer playoffs.

Today we would play her team again—the final game of the basketball season—to decide who had the best intramural team in the sixth grade.

I burst out of my last class the way our dog explodes from the car after a drive. I ran to the locker room and changed. My team met to discuss our strategy.

"Let's have Tina shadow Kerry the entire game," said Mary. "With Tina's long arms in her face, Kerry might be forced to pass."

Just then, Jill came into the gym and ran over to us. I didn't think she would figure much in the game. Jill was awkward and slow. I'd thrown her a pass in one game and it just hit her in the chest. She didn't put her hands up or anything.

As captain, I had to decide who started and how long everyone played. The gym teacher, Mr. Buckner, said it would build character for the captains to make these decisions. It's hard when all the girls are your friends.

"I promise everyone will play at least one quarter," I said.

"Does that include 'Ace'?" Tina asked, nodding toward Jill. Some of the girls laughed. Jill blushed and tucked in her shirt.

"Everyone," I said. I glared at Tina, but if the score were really close, I wasn't sure I'd be able to keep my promise.

We did our warm-up drills, then Mr. Buckner blew his whistle and the starters ran onto the court.

Kerry's team had bought new red jerseys for this championship game. Of course Kerry wore number 1. We didn't have uniforms, but I didn't care, because I knew we had a good team.

The game was fast from the tap, with a lot of running and bumping and back-and-forth scoring. Kerry's team was bigger and they were penetrating more, but we were hitting the outside shots. At half time it was all even at 22, but Kerry was shooting really well. She would be hard to stop late in the game. Just as she'd been in flag football. And soccer.

The score stayed close throughout the second half. Midway through the fourth quarter, Kerry drove in for a lay-up and caught Mary in the face with an elbow.

"Are you all right?" I asked.

"I think so," Mary said, but her eyes looked a little funny. I looked toward the bench.

"Let's go, Jill," I called.

"Me?" she said, looking around as if there were another Jill nearby. Kerry laughed.

"Yeah," I said. "Cover number 40."

Jill nodded, trying to look calm.

The game got a little rougher as the final minutes ticked away. Kerry was taking most of her team's shots. They had the lead, but we kept it close.

With half a minute to go, I hit a jumper that got us to within one point—39-38. "Tough defense now!" I shouted. "Let's get the ball back."

Kerry took the inbound pass and started dribbling up the court. Kerry's teammates were yelling for the ball.

"It's under control," Kerry said as she swerved, dribbling right between Tina and me.

I made a lunge for the ball, and Tina, with her long arms, came around the other side and swiped it. I broke to the basket and Tina fed me the ball, but two defenders raced over to cover me.

Time was running out. I pivoted for an off-balance shot and caught a glimpse of Jill standing underneath the basket. I didn't know if she'd been left there from the previous play, but there she was, completely open.

I elbowed my way between the two defenders and bounced the ball to Jill. She grabbed it hard— you could hear the slap of her hands on the ball. She turned to the basket and heaved the ball up over her head, barely lifting her feet from the floor.

I couldn't watch, but I listened to the ball hitting the rim of the basket in that heavy, dead way that tells you it missed.

Mr. Buckner blew his whistle. The game was over.

Kerry's team shouted in triumph. Jill stood under the basket, in the same place she'd taken the shot, with her arms at her sides and her head hanging down. I looked at Kerry's team, leaping and yelling and laughing. Then I grabbed Jill's arm and said, "Nice try."

Kerry walked past me, over to Jill.

"Good game," Kerry said. Then she shook my hand and said, "Nice pass. That was the right play." She turned and walked toward the locker room. The big number 1 was creased and stuck to Kerry's back with sweat. Jill turned to me with a big smile.

"Softball season starts next week," she said.

"That's right," I said and smiled back.

The Fish-finder

By Sandra Beswetherick

My new friend Zack is wild about fishing, even more than I am. He and his dad own a sleek, expensive bass boat with a motor that rockets it from one end of the lake to the other in no time flat, a dozen high-tech rods and reels, and an electronic, depth-sounding fish-finder.

I don't blame Zack for being surprised when he finds me registering for the fishing derby, too. "You're entering?" he asks.

"Uh-huh."

"But all you have is that little boat and a motor that barely keeps it moving."

"That's all," I agree.

"And your fishing gear . . ."

"Consists of your basic retail model." I hold up the only rod and reel I own.

Zack pats my shoulder, shaking his head. It's his way of telling me I don't stand a chance of winning this derby. "You don't even have a fish-finder," he says.

"I wouldn't say that."

"Since when have you had a fish-finder?"

"I've had one for a few years now," I tell him.

"Oh, yeah?" Zack doesn't know whether he believes me or not.

"But it isn't anything like yours," I say, to make him feel better.

The day of the derby arrives. As the sun clears the trees, my grandfather and I start put-putting across the water in our boat. When we pass the public dock, the line of pickup trucks pulling boat trailers seems two miles long. The drivers are waiting to launch.

We don't get far up the lake before a boat roars past, almost swamping us. Then it spins on a dime, spraying a curtain of water, and pulls along-side, motor rumbling.

"Hi," says Zack.

"Hi," I say back.

"How'd you get on the lake so fast?" Zack asks. "I didn't see you anywhere near the dock."

"Grandad knew a spot up the channel, big enough to launch our boat." I nod at my grandfather sitting in the stern by the motor.

"This is my friend Zack, Grandad."

Grandad nods to Zack. "Pleased to meet you." Then he nods to Zack's dad, Mr. Emerson. "That's quite some ship you've got there." Grandad's being polite. He told me once that he'd have to be drowning before anyone could drag him onto an aircraft carrier like the Emersons'.

I can tell that Mr. Emerson feels the same way about our boat. "Yes. And it's . . . uh . . . a quaint little outfit you've got there," he says.

"Where's your fish-finder?" Zack asks.

"It's on board," I tell him.

"Right on board," Grandad echoes.

Zack's eyes shift to the tarp-covered object at Grandad's feet.

Mr. Emerson raises an eyebrow. "Exactly where are you boys heading?" he asks.

"Thought we'd try our luck over there." Grandad points toward the opposite shore and a small cove, green with reeds poking up through the water.

Mr. Emerson snorts. "No fish-finder in the world would work there. The water's too shallow and too choked with weeds for any finder to register a proper image."

"Our fish-finder will work OK," I say.

"It's always worked before," Grandad adds.

When Zack wrinkles his forehead, I explain that our fish-finder is unusually sophisticated and generally very reliable.

"When have you ever known it to be unreliable?" Grandad demands, glaring at me and tapping his fingers on the tarp.

Mr. Emerson chuckles. "Well, it must be some fish-finder if, in addition to locating the fish, it can keep your lines from tangling in that swamp. All anyone would hook over there is weeds."

"It's some fish-finder, all right," I tell him.

Zack looks at us as though we'd been rocking in our boat too long.

"We'd better go, Zack, if we want to win this derby." Mr. Emerson revs the engine a couple of times. "There's no sign of fish here." He jerks his thumb at their fish-finder. The plateaus and valleys of the lake bottom directly beneath their boat are profiled on the screen in black. I don't see any red fish-blips.

As they rocket away, Zack shouts over his

shoulder, "Good luck!" as if it's something we desperately need.

A blue heron is the only one fishing the cove when we nose our way in. Grandad stops the engine about fifteen feet from the reedbed. "Time to put the old fish-finder to work," he says with a laugh, ready to bust. He flips back the tarp and raises the lid.

"Grape juice or apple?" he asks.

"Grape."

The first thing I'm going to do with the prize money is buy a new cooler, even though Grandad insists this one works fine as long as we keep it covered.

"Now," Grandad says, after taking a sip of juice. "See that clump of reeds over to your left? Right in there."

"Are you sure?"

"How long have I been fishing this lake?"

"All your life," I say.

"The fish that's going to win the derby is hiding in there. Cast a foot out from the weeds and lure him clear. Then hook him hard and fast, so he won't be ducking back in."

When Zack sees the size of our winning fish, his eyes practically pop out of his face.

"Wow!" he says, staring at the fish. "Do you

think, maybe sometime, my dad and I could bor-
row your fish-finder?"

Grandad starts coughing and sputtering.

"There's only one problem, Zack," I explain.
"This fish-finder is so temperamental, it refuses to
work on any boat but ours."

The Running Machine

By Margaret Walden Froehlich

Be a speed machine, Gina. Arms driving legs, legs driving feet. Confident and fast. That's what Coach keeps telling me. That's what she's been telling me all season.

I'm not a finely tuned machine, but I am a pretty good cross-country runner. Top runner on the Macedo Middle School girls' team, in fact.

But I can already feel the butterflies in my stomach this morning. Today is the day of the league championship, the day I compete against

"Flash," oops, I mean Karyn Snyder. Believe me, Karyn *does* run like a well-oiled machine.

I dress and pack my gym bag. I stretch for a minute, then sprint out of my room and down the hall. *Knees up, knees high, lift, lift!* Like pistons in an engine, I tell myself.

From downstairs I hear, "Gina, take it easy up there or the ceiling will fall!"

"Sorry, Mom," I call as I hurry down the stairs. "I'm trying to keep my focus for the race."

Mom hugs me. "You'll do fine," she says.

I pantomime a case of the ultimate jitters and go into the kitchen, where my little sister is practicing her "sport."

Whoomp! Four-year-old Emmy collides with me. She got roller skates recently. She spends more time on her knees than she does skating, but she would wear her skates to bed if Mom let her.

I steady Emmy and she takes off. "This is fun!" she cries.

As I nibble toast, I picture Karyn Snyder fueling up—excuse me, eating her breakfast.

"We'll be there rooting for you," Mom promises as I head for the school bus. Emmy calls, "Have fun, Gina!" A second "Have fun!" explodes, because at that moment her feet go zippity-do-dah.

After homeroom, I head for English class. Does Karyn Snyder need two minutes to get from homeroom to English? No, she probably arrives in class fifteen seconds before she leaves homeroom. (I might be carrying this "machine" thing too far.)

I can't eat lunch—hamburgers, which I adore—because the butterflies in my stomach are as big as blimps.

By 2:30, when we board the bus to head for the race, my legs feel like boiled string. I try to focus on what Coach Drennan is saying: "You all have had such a *great* season! We can win today. Now, listen up. Pretend you're speed machines; pretend those arms are driving those legs, are driving those feet. Lean forward, and open your stride on the downhills. Save your sprint for the finish."

We reach the school field in Unionville, and my teammates rocket out of the bus. Coach Drennan pulls me aside. "Gina, you have a real chance to win this race."

"What about Karyn Snyder?" I say. "She beat me easily last time."

"But that was early in the season on a flat course," Coach says. "I know Karyn's fast, but she has trouble on hilly courses like this one. Use your arms to drive yourself up those hills. Think of yourself as . . ."

". . . a machine," I say. I take a deep breath and totter off the bus.

I am so nervous about the race that I don't even search the field for my parents and little sister. Usually I make a complete fool of myself waving at my family.

We join the runners from the nine other schools to jog the one-and-a-half-mile course, most of it through hilly woods and fields. We do that to get warmed up and to make sure no one makes a wrong turn during the race. I keep my eyes on Karyn Snyder.

All too soon we take our positions at the starting line. Suddenly, a little voice pipes, "Hey, Gina! Have fun!"

The loudspeaker crackles, *"On your marks, get set . . ."*

I pour on power as the starter's whistle blares. If I get in front of the pack, I can concentrate on running like a machine. *Lean forward, drive your arms, don't weave.* I do everything Coach says, but Karyn pulls even on the first downhill slope.

· We run shoulder to shoulder, stride for stride. Sweat streams down my face. I'll drive forward on the hills and outdistance her, I promise myself.

On the next hill, I pull ahead of Karyn, but then on the level I lose ground and can't make it up. I fall a few strides behind; my legs are starting to hurt.

I wish my feet were wheels so I could coast. I think of Emmy and my tension eases. I move up again, alongside Karyn. No one else is close.

Near the finish, Karyn breaks into a sprint and builds a lead. I grit my teeth; my muscles scream as I try to overtake her. But every ounce of strength I have is not enough. Karyn wins.

After the race, I hug Karyn and congratulate her. I'm laughing and crying. As Karyn hugs me, she's laughing and crying, too.

Know something? Machines don't cry. What's more, they don't laugh! And they don't hug! Even if I didn't win, it makes me feel good to have tried my best.

Where's Emmy? I've got to tell her that racing is fun!

Queen
of the
Court

By Dori Hillestad Butler

"Stacy!" my coach called. "Court 5. Ten minutes."

"OK!" I replied. I was banking the ball off a wall, practicing my backhand. *Zing-plop, zing-plop, zing-plop, whoosh!* "Darn!"

As I ran to retrieve my ball, I caught a glimpse of Laura Talbott on Court 4. Laura was from Longmeadow. Everybody said she was Queen of the Courts. But as I pressed my forehead against the fence and watched, I wasn't impressed. Nearly every ball she hit went out of bounds.

A girl who reeked of grape bubblegum came up beside me. "Laura's off today," she said as she cracked her gum in my ear. She wore a Longmeadow shirt just like Laura's. "It's because her mom died," the girl went on. "This is her first meet since it happened."

"Oh!" I said.

I felt funny watching her after that, so I went back to my wall and my backhand. When it was time for my match, Laura was dragging herself from her court.

I never would have guessed she'd won her match if her friend hadn't cracked her gum and yelled, "Way to go, Laura!"

Laura shrugged. She didn't seem to care that she'd won. I wondered what she was even doing here. This wasn't a big meet, just the four local schools—Maple Valley, Longmeadow, Southwest, and my own, Plainview.

"Over here, Stacy," my coach waved me over to Court 5. I shook hands with my opponent, a girl from Maple Valley, and put Laura out of my head.

The girl from Maple Valley and I were pretty evenly matched. She had a great serve, but almost no backhand. I had a pretty good backhand, but an awful serve. In the end, I won three out of five games, which took the match.

As I walked off the court, I saw Laura's friend talking to a group of girls from Southwest. "It's been really hard for Laura since her mom died," she said as she cracked her gum. I couldn't hear the rest of it, but the redhead from Southwest nodded a lot.

I watched as the redhead jogged over to Court 3. Laura was already there. She paced back and forth.

The Southwest girls were tough. As tough as Laura was supposed to be. But as I watched the first game between Laura and the redhead, I didn't think either one was playing very tough. Balls flew randomly all over the court.

I continued with my own games. By noon I had won four matches. I was having a great day.

Apparently, so was Laura. When I checked the stats, I saw she'd won all her matches. She must have put her problems out of her mind and started concentrating on her game.

I checked the board to see who I was playing next. Laura Talbott! Butterflies swarmed in my stomach. I'd never played anybody as good as Laura before.

I took a few deep breaths and went out to the court. The smell of grape bubblegum filled the air. "Remember, Laura wants to win for her mom," said a voice behind me.

"Huh?" I spun around.

Laura's friend was leaning against the fence. She blew a huge bubble then sucked it back in. "You're going to let her win, aren't you?"

Let her win? Was that why Laura was doing so well? People were letting her win?

I glanced across the court at Laura. She was off in her own little world, bouncing a tennis ball.

I sighed. I didn't know what to do. I didn't want to let her win. But if I didn't let her win, what kind of person was I? Laura wanted to win *for her mom*.

Laura and I volleyed for the serve. She got it.

"Love-love," she called as she stretched up and served. The ball flew over my head and landed about a foot past the line. She frowned.

She tried again. This time the ball bounced right in front of me. I slammed it into the net. Laura's friend nodded her approval.

I hit the next ball into the net, too. And I hit the ball out after that. Before I knew it, Laura had won the first game. But I wasn't very proud of myself for the way I was playing.

We switched sides and a new game began.

Laura hardly moved. She hit the ball when it came to her, but she didn't go after it. She wasn't trying any harder than I was.

This was stupid. Why was I letting her win if she wasn't even going to try?

The next time the ball came to me, I slammed it back so hard she had to jump out of the way. Even from this distance I could see her eyes widen with surprise.

I scored the rest of the points in that game, which left me down 1-2 for the match. But I could catch up.

Once I started playing for real, Laura did, too. The sadness on her face was replaced with a look of determination. But it wasn't enough. I won the match 3-2.

"Good game," said Laura as we shook hands.

"Yeah," I said. I felt a little funny about winning, especially when her friend glared at me from the sidelines.

"Maybe we'll get to play again sometime," I told Laura.

Her face brightened. "I'd like that," she said. She even smiled. It was her first smile of the day. I wonder if her friend noticed?

ON THE RIGHT TRACK

By Isobel V. Morin

Lucas squirmed around on the bleacher seat and smiled at his friend, Andy Tyler. Mr. Schwartz, the coach of the school track team, was finishing his talk about the team. "Remember that it doesn't matter how fast you can run," the coach said. "There is room on the team for anyone who's willing to work hard and do his best."

As the two boys walked back to their classroom, Lucas asked Andy, "Going to sign up for the track team with me? It will be a good way for you to get to know people at this school."

Andy and Lucas were next-door neighbors, but they had never gone to school together before. Andy had just transferred to Lucas's school from a special school for children with physical handicaps. Andy had cerebral palsy, a condition that can affect people's speech, movement, and in some cases, their ability to think. Andy was lucky, though. The condition had put some limits on his ability to walk and talk but had left his mind unaffected.

Before answering Lucas, Andy pressed his lips together and swallowed. He dabbed at his mouth with a balled-up tissue. Forming his words slowly and carefully, he said, "I'm not sure. It would be fun to try, but maybe the others wouldn't want me on the team."

"I don't think that will happen," Lucas said. "When the school board decided to move some children from your school to ours, our principal gave a talk to explain the move. We all promised to welcome the newcomers and to look at what they *can* do instead of what they can't do. Besides, if anyone gives you trouble, I'll . . . "

Lucas made a fist and shook it at Andy, who laughed and said, "OK, I'll try it."

Andy had a hard time keeping up with the others during the practice runs. He often struggled to make it to the finish line. The other team members did their best to encourage him, however, just as Lucas had predicted.

At the track meets Lucas, who was easily the fastest runner on the team, usually came in first. Andy, on the other hand, always finished a distant last. When Andy finally crossed the finish line, the team cheered as loudly for him as they did for anyone else, though. Sometimes Andy would joke about it, referring to himself as the team's caboose or saying, "I guess they're glad that the race is finally over."

During one track meet, Coach Schwartz ran over to Lucas as he crossed the finish line. "You broke a school record," the coach yelled as he pumped Lucas's hand.

Andy lumbered over to Lucas and slapped him on the back. "Way to go, champ!" he shouted. Then, smiling broadly, Andy added, "I dropped a half second off my best time. Not bad, huh?"

"Not bad at all. In fact, that is pretty good," Lucas replied.

By the end of the track season, Lucas had gathered a fistful of first-place ribbons, plus a few special ribbons for breaking school records. As Lucas tacked his latest blue ribbons onto his bulletin board, Andy said, "You're a shoo-in to win the prize for Most Valuable Player. You should win it in a walk—I mean, a run."

Both boys laughed. Then Lucas said, "And you might win the prize for Most Improved Player. Your times have come down a lot since the season began."

On the day of the sports awards, Lucas could hardly sit still while the prizes were announced. One by one, the trophies were handed out. At last it was the track team's turn. Coach Schwartz rose and picked up a trophy.

"The prize for Most Improved Player goes to Michael O'Dowd."

Lucas hoped Andy wasn't too disappointed. He sneaked a peek at his friend. Andy was smiling and clapping his hands.

The coach reached for the next trophy—the one for Most Valuable Player. Lucas sat on the edge of the seat, ready to go and get his prize. He fidgeted as the coach began to speak. *Hurry up and get to the winner's name*, he mentally urged Coach Schwartz.

"It is never easy to pick the most valuable player," the coach began, "But this year it was especially hard. Two runners stood out. They are both exceptional. Unfortunately, we have only one award. My choice for Most Valuable Player is Andy Tyler."

Lucas stifled a gasp of disbelief. He could feel his face flushing. He couldn't help wondering what was so valuable about a last-place runner. Then he scolded himself. *Andy is your best friend. You should be glad for him.* Lucas's hands felt like lumps of lead, but he managed to clap hard for Andy.

Coach Schwartz motioned for silence. "You're probably wondering why I didn't choose Lucas Lee for Most Valuable Player. I almost did. Lucas is one of the best runners this school has ever had. He deserves a big round of applause for that."

When the applause died down, Coach Schwartz continued. "Andy can't run fast, but he's a winner. Most of you know that Andy has cerebral palsy. That means his brain doesn't always send the right signals to the rest of his body. The doctors discovered the condition when Andy was a baby. For a long time they thought he would never learn to walk. As you can see, Andy showed them that they were wrong. Andy not only learned to walk—he learned to run."

Coach Schwartz shook Andy's hand as he gave him the trophy. "Congratulations, Andy. You're an inspiration to all of us."

As soon as the assembly was over, Andy slipped out of his seat and headed for the door. Lucas hurried after his friend, calling out, "Wait for me."

Andy kept walking.

Lucas ran past him and stood in front of him, blocking his path. Planting his hands on his hips, he demanded, "What's wrong with you?"

Andy stared at the floor. He whispered, "I'm sorry, Lucas. I took your trophy away from you."

"No, you didn't. It's yours. You earned it. You showed us what people can do if they put their minds to it. You're a real champ."

A smile spread over Andy's face. He swallowed hard and said, "So are you!"

Stuck
in
Goal

By David Dayen

Brett bent over and picked at a blade of grass. Far down the field, he could barely see his teammates attacking the opposing goal. Brett's younger brother, Nathan, stood behind the net. Nathan was too young to play on the league, but he was a great coach. And the way Nathan stood, poised and attentive, made him look more like the goalie than Brett.

"Hey, Brett, look out for their wingman. He's trying to sneak up the side," Nathan said.

"How can you tell, Nathan? They're all so far away, it'll take them a week to get to this end." Brett kicked at the dirt in front of the goal crease with his cleats. Most of the time Brett would start on offense, making passes and scoring goals. He scored twice for the Sockers in the first half of today's game. But Coach Conagher knew Brett was his best athlete. Whenever the team got a lead, he'd send Brett in to play goalie. Now it was nearly the end of the game, and Brett had been standing by his net alone most of the time. He sighed. At least he'd have Nathan to talk with.

"Come on, Brett, don't let your guard down," Nathan warned.

Brett turned around to face his brother. "How could I let my guard down when it has never been up? This is too easy! All I do is stand here. I don't even have to stand." Brett sat down with his back to the action. "See, Nathan, I could just sit here all game."

"Uh, Brett, I don't think you should—"

"Why not? I could use a rest. It doesn't matter anyway." Brett squirmed around to get comfortable on the hard ground. He shut his eyes, imagining himself controlling the ball, running up the field, kicking the ball into the corner of the net, just past the Buccaneer goalie. Another goal! The crowd was cheering, his friends were smacking him on the back . . .

"Ummmm, Brett . . . I think you should get up."

"Don't worry about it, Nathan," Brett said, but as he spoke he heard a couple of his teammates screaming. He opened his eyes and turned his head to check out the commotion. The Buccaneer's center had stolen the ball, and he passed it up to his wingman. The wingman was streaking down the left sideline on a breakaway!

Brett quickly sprang to his feet, dusting off his uniform.

"Cover the short side of the net, or else he'll sneak it by you!" Nathan urged.

Brett crouched low and shifted toward the left goalpost, feeling for it with his left hand. He never took his eyes off the wingman. By now the Buccaneer player had almost reached the goal. Brett felt a lump in his throat. He figured the wingman would aim for the other side of the net to try to score. So Brett leaned away from the goalpost just as the Buccaneer kicked the ball in that direction. Brett knew he would have to jump for it. He stretched out as far as he could, his hands grabbing at air. With a final effort, Brett snatched the ball while falling to earth. He made the save!

"Hurry up, Brett! Kick it up the side!" Nathan

implored. But Brett could not focus on his brother's words. He stood up and looked around for one of his teammates. The ball felt heavy in his sweaty hands. Finally, he saw his best friend on the team, Charlie, coming toward the ball from the center of the field. There were a couple of Buccaneer players out there as well. Brett didn't stop to think. He just wanted to get rid of the ball. He rolled the ball out toward Charlie, turned around and ran back to the goal area.

"Brett, turn around! *Quick*!" A Buccaneer girl had taken the ball. Brett had rolled it right to her. Brett only heard his brother in time to look back and see the ball flash right past him. Goal!

On the sidelines, the girl's mother jumped up and down wildly. "Oh my goodness! She scored! She never scored before! Look at my baby!" The little girl beamed. Her teammates picked her up and carried her to the sidelines, hollering and cheering all the way.

Brett kept his head down as he retrieved the ball from the net. He couldn't look at anybody. Charlie just glared at Brett when he came over to get the ball. "What were you sitting down for? Good job. Now the game's tied because of you."

Brett didn't think that was fair. After all, he had scored twice in the first half. And he made the great save earlier. How come everybody thought he cost the team the game? Nathan walked over to Brett. "You'll do better next time. Just don't get caught with your guard down!"

"But Nathan, I scored for the team before. I helped them to get ahead in this game."

"Yeah, but this time the coach wasn't asking you to score. All you had to do was kick it up the side. You know that."

The Sockers started their offensive possession. But a Buccaneer player stole the ball again, and he controlled it. Three Buccaneers moved toward the goal zone. Brett was not sitting down now. He watched the movement of the ball. Suddenly, a Buccaneer took a shot. Brett blocked it with his body. The ball bounced out to another Buccaneer. He took a close-in shot, but Brett leaped to his left and caught the ball in midflight.

Now Brett had to get the ball out of his zone. His eyes met Charlie's, and he knew instantly what to do. They had worked on this maneuver in practice. Brett walked up as if he were going to roll the ball to the side. As the Buccaneers prepared for this, Charlie scooted toward midfield. Brett faked the roll and instead drop-kicked the ball high in the air. Charlie got the ball in stride and was flying right toward the Buccaneer net!

Though Brett was far away from Charlie, he smiled and cheered as though he were right next to him.

"Great job, Brett!" Nathan yelled. Brett never felt happier than at that moment—not even when he scored a goal—not ever.